This **TWO HOOTS** book belongs to

For my Mooncat, Freya

First published 2021 by Two Hoots
an imprint of Pan Macmillan,
The Smithson, 6 Briset Street, London EC1M 5NR
EU representative: Macmillan Publishers Ireland Ltd, 1st Floor,
The Liffey Trust Centre, 117–126 Sheriff Street Upper, Dublin 1, D01 YC43
Associated companies throughout the world
www.panmacmillan.com

ISBN: 978-1-5290-4868-1

Text and Illustration copyright © Lydia Corry 2021
Moral rights asserted.

All rights reserved. No part of this publication may be reproduced, stored
in or introduced into a retrieval system, or transmitted, in any form, or by
any means (electronic, mechanical, photocopying, recording or otherwise)
without the prior written permission of the publisher.

5 7 9 8 6

A CIP catalogue record for this book is available from the British Library.

Printed in China.

The illustrations in this book were created using watercolour, pencil,
ink and gouache on a heavy hot pressed paper.
Children's artwork pages 24-25 by Sylvie (aged 5).

www.twohootsbooks.com

Mooncat
and me

LYDIA CORRY

TWO HOOTS

My name is Pearl.
My number one animal is a cat.
I like swimming, and I *really*
like strawberry ice cream
with one sprinkle on top.

But I do NOT like moving house.

And I'm sure I will definitely not like starting a new school.

I won't know anybody there, and nobody will know me.

The new flat felt empty and strange.

I stared out of my window, listening to the cars and trucks rattling past and the alley cats meowing at the moon.

Mum said it will start to feel normal soon, but I'm not sure she's right.

"Shall we go out exploring today?"
Mum asked the next morning.

But I shook my head.
Explorers are supposed
to be big and bold and
brave, I thought.

Then I looked up and all of a sudden there he was. Huge, fluffy, and as bright as the moon, with twinkling, smiling eyes. I couldn't believe it.

I called him Mooncat and invited him in for breakfast.

Mum didn't seem to mind . . .

. . . but I decided it might be a good idea to go out exploring after all.

Outside, everything seemed so big and so loud.

But Mooncat was there.

We rode a bus across town, past buildings that scraped the sky.

I did feel a bit small, but Mooncat was there.

When we got to the swimming pool, we kept watch for sharks and sea monsters in mysterious lagoons. I did feel a teeny bit shy, but Mooncat was there.

After lunch, we went to the park. Mooncat and I built shelters out of sticks and leaves and lived in them all afternoon.

I taught Mooncat how not to step on the lines,

and Mooncat showed me how to jump really high!

And when it was time to go home, Mooncat and I prowled through dark tangled forests full of dangerous wild beasts.

What an amazing day we'd had!

To my surprise, I realized I was feeling a little bit bigger, a little bit bolder, and quite a lot braver!

The next day Mum helped me get ready for school.

But when I got to school, I didn't know anybody, and nobody knew me.

Then I heard a voice saying hello.

Her name was Mavis. I asked her what her favourite flavour of ice cream was. I'd never heard of tutti frutti, but it sounded brilliant.

Soon I knew everybody, and everybody knew me.

I was having so much fun, I couldn't believe when it was home time already.

On the way home we got ice cream.

I had tutti frutti with just one sprinkle on top. I'd never tasted anything like it before.

I had so much to tell Mum about the new friends I'd made, that I didn't notice Mooncat wasn't there.

That night I stared out of my window at the thousands of twinkling lights. They reminded me of Mooncat's smiling eyes. Where could he be?

Suddenly I was floating up   and   up   and   up.

Mooncat had been there all along.